Holly the Christmas Fairy was originally published
as a Rainbow Magic special. This version has
been specially adapted for developing readers
in conjunction with a Reading Consultant.

Special thanks to
Narinder Dhami
and Sarah Levison

ORCHARD BOOKS

This story published in Great Britain in 2004 by Orchard Books
This Early Reader edition published in 2017 by The Watts Publishing Group

1 3 5 7 9 10 8 6 4 2

© 2017 Rainbow Magic Limited.
© 2017 HIT Entertainment Limited.
Illustrations © Orchard Books 2017

HiT entertainment

A CIP catalogue record for this book is available from the British Library.

ISBN 978 1 40834 440 8

Printed in China

MIX
Paper from
responsible sources
FSC
www.fsc.org
FSC® C104740

The paper and board used in this book are made from wood from responsible sources.

Orchard Books
An imprint of Hachette Children's Group
Part of The Watts Publishing Group Limited
Carmelite House, 50 Victoria Embankment, London EC4Y 0DZ

An Hachette UK Company
www.hachette.co.uk
www.hachettechildrens.co.uk

Holly
the Christmas
Fairy

Daisy Meadows

ORCHARD

www.rainbowmagic.co.uk

Hillfields Farm

Christmas
Trees

HILLFIELDS
FARM

Tippington
Town

Santa's Cabin

RAINBOW SHOPPING CENTRE

Shopping Centre

Rachel's House

Contents

Story One

Christmas Countdown

Chapter One

Three Days Until Christmas

It was the Christmas holidays
and best friends Rachel
Walker and Kirsty Tate were
at Rachel's house.

"Only three days to go until
Christmas!" smiled Kirsty,
playing with her golden locket.
Both girls wore magical lockets.

They had been a present from their very special friends, the Rainbow Magic fairies!

Mrs Walker came into the room. "Hello, girls! We're going to choose a Christmas tree later. Do you want to fetch the decorations from the garage?"

The girls ran to get the decorations. But as Rachel reached up for a box her locket burst open, scattering fairy dust everywhere!

"Kirsty!" Rachel cried as both girls slowly started to shrink.

"We must be on our way to Fairyland!"

When the girls landed by the Fairyland Palace a moment later, Queen Titania came towards them. "Our magic made your locket open," she said. "I'm afraid we need your help again!"

A pretty little fairy came towards the girls. She had long, wavy dark hair and wore a red dress with a furry hood.

"Hello," she said sadly. "I'm Holly the Christmas Fairy. It's my job to make sure that Christmas is as sparkly and happy as possible."

"But Jack Frost is causing trouble," sighed Queen Titania. "We'll show you what happened." She waved her wand over a pool of water. Pictures began to appear on the surface.

Kirsty and Rachel saw a log cabin surrounded by deep snow. Outside was a beautiful sleigh, sparkling with magic.

"That's Santa's workshop, and his sleigh!" Holly whispered to the girls.

Eight reindeer were harnessed to the sleigh. Lots of elves were filling it with presents. But then the spiky figure of Jack Frost appeared!

Jack Frost ran over to the

sleigh and jumped in. It lifted off the ground and zoomed away into the starry night sky. The picture in the pool faded away.

"We must find Santa's sleigh, or Christmas will be ruined," said the queen. "There are three special presents on that sleigh."

"We'll find the sleigh and the presents," the girls cried.

The queen gave the girls a little bag. Inside was a golden crown. "If you put this crown on Jack Frost's head, he will be brought back to Fairyland.

Now, it's time for you to go home. Holly will come and see you soon!" The queen sent a shower of fairy dust over the girls.

The two best friends smiled at each other. They were about to start another magical adventure!

Chapter Two

A Very Special Tree

That evening, Kirsty and
Rachel went with Mr and
Mrs Walker to a farm to choose
the Christmas tree. Buttons the
dog came too!

Rachel soon spotted a
beautiful tree. Holly the fairy
appeared in the branches!

Just then there was a shout from Mrs Walker, and Buttons dashed past the girls, barking loudly.

"Stop him, girls!" cried Mrs Walker.

"We will!" Rachel called.

Holly fluttered into Kirsty's pocket and the girls ran after Buttons. He was racing towards an old barn. Kirsty spotted a shadow in front of them with a pointed nose and big feet. It rushed into the barn.

"Oh!" Kirsty gasped. "I think Buttons is chasing one of Jack Frost's goblins!"

Rachel tied Buttons up outside the barn and the girls peeped inside. There were large open doors at the opposite end of the barn. A sparkling trail led outside and right up into the sky. At the far end of the trail, they spotted Santa's sleigh disappearing into the distance!

"We've just missed Jack Frost," said Kirsty, disappointed.

Rachel noticed that the barn had wrapping paper scattered everywhere. "Mean Jack Frost has been opening Santa's presents!" she said crossly.

Just then the girls spotted two goblins. They were squabbling over a super-sparkly present.

"Look!" cried Kirsty. "It must be one of the special presents the queen asked us to find."

"The other two presents must still be on the sleigh," Holly said.

"How are we going to get the present?" Rachel whispered.

Kirsty thought hard. "I've got an idea," she said. "Holly, could you magic up the smell of mince pies?"

"Of course," Holly replied.

"We'll tell the greedy goblins there's a big plate of mince pies in the hayloft," Kirsty went on.

"They'll have to put the present down to climb into the hayloft and then we'll be able to grab the present!"

"Great idea!" said Holly. "One magic smell of hot mince pies coming up!" And she flew towards the goblins.

Rachel and Kirsty watched anxiously as Holly fluttered over the goblins' heads. Would their plan work …?

Chapter Three

Greedy Goblins!

Holly waved her wand.
Moments later the delicious
smell of mince pies drifted
around the barn.

The goblins sniffed.

"Fresh mince pies, up in the
hayloft!" Holly called. "Help
yourselves."

"Mince pies! Yum!" shouted the goblins. They threw the present down on a pile of straw and scrambled up the ladder.

When they had reached the top, the girls dashed into the barn and Kirsty picked up the parcel.

Suddenly there was a shout from the goblins. "There aren't

any mince pies here! We've been tricked!"

"Quick!" gasped Holly. "Let's get out of here!"

The girls and Holly ran to the door as the goblins tumbled down the ladder.

Outside the barn Rachel untied Buttons. The goblins appeared in the doorway and ran towards her. But Buttons began to bark loudly and the two terrified creatures shot back into the barn and slammed the door.

"Good dog!" said Rachel, patting Buttons.

"Hurrah! We've found one special present." Holly beamed. "Thank you so much!"

"We'll see you again soon,"

Rachel called, as Holly fluttered up into the sky.

"I'll be back as soon as I find out where Jack Frost is now!" Holly promised.

Rachel and Kirsty hurried back to the farm. Rachel's mum and dad were tying the Christmas tree to the roof of the car.

"Let's head home for mince pies and hot chocolate," said Rachel's mum, as they climbed into the car.

Rachel and Kirsty grinned at each other.

"I think Buttons deserves a mince pie too," Kirsty whispered to her friend. "After all, he was the one who led us to the goblins and the first present."

"Woof!" Buttons agreed.

"Yes, and our fairy adventures aren't over yet," Rachel said. "We still have to save the sleigh and find two presents!"

Story Two

Search for the Sleigh

Chapter One

A Special Shopping Trip

The next morning the girls were getting ready to go Christmas shopping with Rachel's mum.

"I hope we can find Jack Frost and Santa's sleigh today," said Kirsty.

Rachel nodded in agreement. "Yes. Then we can really start

to enjoy Christmas!"

The girls clattered downstairs. Mrs Walker was waiting for them in the hall.

"Don't forget your scarves and gloves," she said. "It's freezing today!" She opened the front door and went to get the car from the garage.

"Doesn't the tree look fantastic?" said Kirsty, looking at the glittering tree in the hall.

Looking closely, Rachel saw a beautiful fairy at the top of the tree. Holly the Christmas Fairy!

Holly flew down
and landed on
Kirsty's shoulder.
"Hello, girls!"
she said in
her tinkly
voice. "I think
something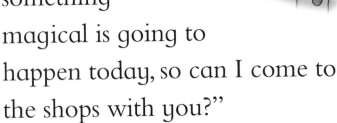
magical is going to
happen today, so can I come to
the shops with you?"

"Of course," Rachel replied
happily. She ran upstairs to
fetch the golden crown given to
them by Queen Titania.

If they could put it on Jack Frost's head, he would be returned to Fairyland to face the king and queen!

Holly fluttered into Kirsty's coat pocket.

When they reached the shopping centre, Mrs Walker arranged to meet the girls by the lifts an hour later. She went to buy some last-minute gifts.

The girls really enjoyed seeing the Christmas displays. Holly peeped out from Kirsty's pocket to see what was going on.

 She was
so tiny,
nobody
spotted
her!

In the
middle of the shopping centre
was Santa's Grotto. It was a
huge white tent covered in lights
and surrounded by fake snow.

Rachel and Kirsty saw a little
girl run out of the grotto to join
her mum. "Santa wasn't very
nice!" she cried. "And he was all
cold and spiky!"

Immediately Rachel's ears pricked up. That didn't sound like Santa at all. But it did sound like someone else they knew … Jack Frost!

Chapter Two

Frosty Father Christmas

"Kirsty!" Rachel said. "I think Jack Frost is inside the grotto, pretending to be Santa!"

"Let's check it out!" Holly piped up from inside Kirsty's pocket.

"Yes, let's slip in round the back and see what's going on," said Kirsty.

The girls quietly tiptoed round to the back of the grotto. Lifting up the tent, they crept inside and hid behind a cluster of rocks.

Gleaming icicles hung from the ceiling, and a big Christmas tree stood in one corner.

And there, wearing a Santa suit, was Jack Frost! He was sitting in Santa's sparkling sleigh. The sleigh was still loaded with presents.

"Bring me another present!" Jack Frost roared.

His goblin servants rushed over and pushed more presents into Jack Frost's greedy hands.

Suddenly Kirsty spotted something. "Look!" she hissed, pointing at the sleigh. "It's one of the special presents!" The shiny parcel was sitting at the back of the sleigh.

"You're right," Holly whispered excitedly.

"But how are we going to get hold of the present without being spotted?" Rachel asked.

"I can distract Jack Frost," smiled Holly. "I'll use my magic to hide inside one of the presents he is opening."

"Good idea!" Rachel declared. "We'll creep up to the back of the sleigh and grab the present."

"And we'll try to put the crown on Jack Frost's head," Kirsty whispered. "Let's go!"

Rachel and Kirsty began to crawl slowly towards the sleigh.

Soon the special present was so close that Kirsty could reach out and touch it!

"Now we just wait for Holly to appear," Rachel whispered, moving closer to Jack Frost so she could put the magic crown on his head.

Jack Frost ripped the paper off another parcel and held up a wooden box. "I wonder what's in here?" he muttered.

Suddenly the lid of the box burst open. Holly shot out in a shower of sparkly red fairy dust!

Jack Frost and his goblins stared at Holly in stunned surprise. Kirsty stretched out her hands and grabbed the special parcel.

"Stop that pesky Christmas Fairy!" Jack Frost shouted.

Chapter Three

Goblins in the Grotto!

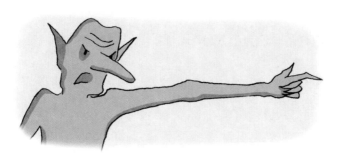

Just then, one of the goblins spotted Rachel and Kirsty. "Look out!" he screeched.

Jack Frost quickly waved his wand and the reindeer galloped off, pulling the sleigh behind them.

"Grab that fairy and those girls!" Jack Frost roared.

"Kirsty! Rachel!" shouted Holly, who was zooming up and away from the goblins. "You've got to get out of here!"

The reindeer galloped out of the tent and flew up into the air. As the sleigh soared out of the

shopping centre, the shoppers looked up in amazement. They began cheering, thinking it was some sort of fabulous Christmas magic show!

Meanwhile, the goblins were closing in on the girls, and Rachel and Kirsty ran away from them. The goblins gave chase, but they kept tripping over their big feet!

The girls rushed out of the grotto. "Quick, Kirsty!" Rachel shouted. "Pull on the support ropes at the back of the tent!"

The two girls began pulling at the ropes with all their might. Suddenly there was a  creaking sound. The large tent wobbled and then fell to the ground, trapping the goblins underneath the canvas!

"We did it!" Kirsty cheered.

Holly zoomed over to land on Kirsty's shoulder. "Thank you

for getting the second present," she smiled.

"It's such a shame Jack Frost got away again," sighed Rachel. "And we don't know where he's gone."

"Oh, yes, we do!" Holly told her excitedly. "I followed the sleigh and spoke to one of the reindeer. He told me that they were taking Jack Frost to his Ice Castle."

The girls shivered. They knew that the Ice Castle was a cold and scary place!

Holly
smiled
happily
at them.
"I will
take this
second
present

back to Fairyland now.
Tomorrow we'll find the
final present and get Santa's
sleigh back!" The little fairy
blew kisses to the girls and
disappeared. The girls went to
the lifts to meet Mrs Walker.

Rachel's mum was already waiting for them and they all headed off to the car. The girls clutched each other's hands. They felt very excited and a little bit nervous about visiting the Ice Castle the next day!

Story Three

The Night Before Christmas

Chapter One

Two Wintry Worlds

Rachel woke up bright and early the next morning. "It's Christmas Eve!" she cried excitedly. She went across to the window and opened the curtains. She gasped in delight when she saw that the garden was covered with sparkling white snow!

Kirsty woke up and they both peered out of the window.

"I can't wait for Christmas," Rachel smiled.

"I know," Kirsty agreed. "We just have to find Father Christmas's sleigh and the last present!"

The two girls threw on their clothes and hurried downstairs for breakfast. Then they pulled on their coats and boots and ran out into the garden.

The girls had fun throwing big snowballs at each other.

But one exploded
in the air,
and Holly
appeared!

"Are you
ready, girls?"
she cried. "It's time
to go to Jack Frost's Ice Castle!"

"We're ready!" Rachel said
bravely. The girls knew that
time would stand still in the
human world whilst they were
away. Kirsty nodded, making
sure that she had the bag
containing the special crown.

Holly waved her wand in the air and moments later the girls found themselves sitting in a tree, staring up at Jack Frost's Ice Castle.

The castle was built from sheets of ice. It looked cold and scary!

The three friends flew off in different directions to look for a way into the castle.

After a few minutes of searching, clever Holly found a trapdoor and used her magic to open the heavy door.

"Let's search for Santa's sleigh," Rachel whispered.

The fairies flew down the winding staircase towards the ground floor of the castle. But they bumped straight into lots of goblin guards! The friends were captured.

"We're going to take you to Jack Frost!" the goblins shouted.

The goblins led the three fairies into the Great Hall. And there was Jack Frost, sitting in Santa's sleigh! The reindeer were still harnessed to it, munching on bales of hay.

Jack Frost looked up at the girls. "You again!" he snarled.

Rachel gasped as she saw the present that Jack Frost was holding. It was the third special present that the queen had asked the girls to find!

Rachel could see that Holly and Kirsty had spotted the present too. But how could they stop Jack Frost from opening it …?

Chapter Two

A Very Clever Plan

Suddenly, Kirsty had an idea.

"Rachel," she whispered.
"Can you distract the goblins
and Jack Frost?"

Rachel nodded. She flapped
her wings and the goblin
holding her loosened his grip.
Rachel zoomed up into the air!

"Seize her!" Jack Frost yelled furiously.

The goblins rushed after Rachel, trying to grab her.

Meanwhile, Kirsty bent down and grabbed a piece of wrapping paper and a purple ribbon from the floor.

She took the bag with the magic crown in it out of her pocket and quickly wrapped it up.

Jack Frost waved his wand, and instantly Rachel's wings froze in mid-air. She fell to the ground, landing on top of two goblins. Luckily she wasn't hurt!

"Now," Jack Frost snapped, "I'm going to open this present!"

"Please, Your Majesty," said Kirsty, stepping forward. "We only came to get this one very special present." She held up the crown, wrapped in the paper.

"It's for the Fairy King. We have to take it to him!"

Jack Frost's eyes lit up as he stared at the parcel. "A present for King Oberon?" he muttered. "It will be mine!"

Jack Frost snatched the present right out of Kirsty's hands.

Kirsty tried not to smile. She knew greedy Jack Frost wouldn't be able to resist taking the present for himself! He ripped the ribbon and paper away to reveal the bag. He put his hand inside and drew out the glittering crown.

"Aha!" he declared triumphantly. "A sparkling new crown for me!" And he put the crown on his head.

Jack Frost vanished!

"Jack Frost has been sent straight to the king and queen," cried Rachel in delight. She jumped into the magic sleigh and picked up the third present.

"Let's get out of this icy place!"

Holly patted one of the reindeer on the head. "Take us back to Santa, please!"

The reindeer began to gallop down the Great Hall. Goblins jumped out of the way as the sleigh picked up speed.

Then it rose into the air, magically passing through the roof of the castle and up into the clouds.

After a few minutes, the girls saw the pretty log cabin that they had first seen in the fairy pool. The sleigh landed and a big group of cheering elves ran over to it.

Rachel and Kirsty gasped with delight as Santa came dashing out of the cabin.

"Are we in time to save Christmas, Santa?" Rachel asked anxiously.

Santa nodded.
"Oh, yes," he
smiled.
"It's
going
to be
a wonderful
Christmas, thanks to you!"

Chapter Three

A Fairy Merry Christmas

"Now," said Santa, "the king
and queen will want to see you.
I'll drop you off on my way to
deliver these gifts."

Rachel and Kirsty couldn't
believe it. They were going
to ride with Santa Claus on
Christmas Eve!

As Santa's sleigh drew closer to Fairyland, there was a shout of welcome from the fairies below. Rachel and Kirsty waved as they saw all their old friends waiting for them.

"We brought you this," Rachel said, handing the third present to the king. Santa waved as his sleigh soared off into the sky.

He had a lot of work to do!

"What's happened to Jack Frost?" asked Rachel.

The king looked stern. "He has had his magic powers taken away from him for a whole year," he explained.

The queen nodded. "But now it's time to celebrate Christmas, and we have special gifts for the three of you."

Kirsty and Rachel gasped in surprise as the queen gave them the two presents they had rescued from Jack Frost!

The king handed Holly the parcel that Rachel had just given him.

There was a new wand for Holly, and when she waved it the sweet sound of tinkling Christmas bells could be heard.

Rachel and Kirsty's presents both contained beautiful fairy dolls!

"These are fairies for the top of your Christmas trees," the queen explained.

Rachel and Kirsty were thrilled to bits.

"But now it's time for you to go home to enjoy Christmas!" the king said.

The girls quickly said their goodbyes.

"Merry Christmas!" called all the fairies as the girls were whizzed away in a haze of magical shimmering sparkles.

Soon they found themselves back in the Walkers' garden.

"We did it, Rachel!" Kirsty laughed. "We saved Christmas!"

The girls ran inside and put Rachel's fairy doll carefully on the top of the tree.

Just then the doorbell rang. It was Kirsty's parents!

"Merry Christmas, girls!"

said Mr and Mrs Tate with a smile, rushing to hug them.

Soon it was time for Kirsty to go home for Christmas. She gave Rachel a huge hug.

"I just know we're going to have the best Christmas ever!" Kirsty whispered.

"I know," Rachel smiled. "And I can't wait to have more magical adventures with my best friend and our special fairy friends!"

The End

**If you enjoyed this story,
you may want to read**

Catherine the
Fashion Princess Fairy
Early Reader

Here's how the story begins ...

One sunny Saturday, best
friends Rachel Walker and
Kirsty Tate were standing in
a crowd outside a beautiful
palace. The girls were visiting
the city for the weekend with
Kirsty's parents and they were

waiting to meet a family friend, Bee, when she had finished work. Bee was a fashion stylist and was inside the palace at that very moment!

Kirsty smiled up at the palace. "It must be fantastic to help the princesses decide what to wear every day," she said.

"Definitely!" agreed Rachel, linking arms with Kirsty.

Everyone loved the three princesses who lived in the palace, but the youngest – Princess Edie – was the girls' favourite!

"It's very different from the Fairyland Palace, isn't it?" Kirsty whispered.

Rachel smiled, thinking of the beautiful pink palace where Queen Titania and King Oberon lived. The girls had been special friends of Fairyland for a long time!

Read
Catherine the Fashion Princess Fairy
Early Reader
to find out
what happens next!

Meet the first
Rainbow Magic fairies

Ruby
the Red Fairy
Daisy Meadows

Amber
the Orange Fairy
Daisy Meadows

Saffron
the Yellow Fairy
Daisy Meadows

Fern
the Green Fairy
Daisy Meadows

Sky
the Blue Fairy
Daisy Meadows

Izzy
the Indigo Fairy
Daisy Meadows

Heather
the Violet Fairy
Daisy Meadows

Can you find one with your name?
There's a fairy book for everyone at
www.rainbowmagicbooks.co.uk

Let the magic begin!

RAINBOW magic™

Become a

Rainbow Magic

fairy friend and be the first to
see sneak peeks of new books.

There are lots of special offers and exclusive
competitions to win sparkly
Rainbow Magic prizes.

Sign up today at
www.rainbowmagicbooks.co.uk